Marvin, the
Blue Pig

First published in 2002 by
Franklin Watts
96 Leonard Street
London
EC2A 4XD

Franklin Watts Australia
56 O'Riordan Street
Alexandria
NSW 2015

A CIP catalogue record for this book is available
from the British Library.

ISBN 0 7496 4473 7 (hbk)
ISBN 0 7496 4619 5 (pbk)

Series Editor: Louise John
Series Advisor: Dr Barrie Wade
Cover Design: Jason Anscomb
Design: Peter Scoulding

Printed in Hong Kong

For Yvonne – KW

Marvin, the Blue Pig

by Karen Wallace and Lisa Williams

FRANKLIN WATTS
LONDON•SYDNEY

Marvin was a sad pig. He wasn't pink like most pigs or even spotty like some pigs.

Marvin was sad because he was a blue pig.

Marvin's best friend in the farmyard was a spotty pig called Esther.

6

Esther danced and told Marvin jokes to try and cheer him up.

Marvin's mother was called
Mrs Pig. She was big, pink and
very wise.

"If you want to be pink, you have to be happy," she said to Marvin. "If you're feeling blue, then you look blue!"

9

One day there was an argument
about who was the best animal in
the farmyard.

"I'm the loveliest," said the cock.

"I'm the strongest," said the horse.

"I'm the woolliest," said the sheep.

"And I'm the milkiest," said the cow.

11

"What are you, Marvin?" asked Mrs Pig. But before Marvin could reply, the cock jumped onto the gate.

"He's the BLUEST!" crowed the cock, and all the animals laughed.

Marvin ran away and locked
himself in his pigsty.

Mrs Pig went to see Marvin.

"Son," she said with a huge sigh,

"if I've told you once, I've told you

a thousand times: if you want to

be pink, you have to be happy!"

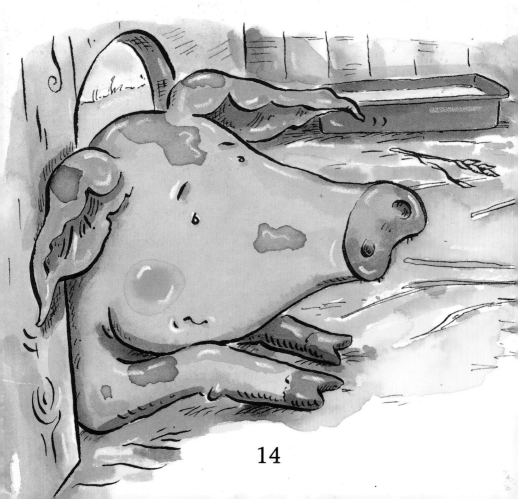

"I've tried," sniffed Marvin.

"Well you'll just have to try harder," replied Mrs Pig, firmly.

Then Esther scratched on the
pigsty door. "I know how you can
turn pink, Marvin," she whispered.

Marvin poked his head out of the door. "How?" he asked.

"I heard the farmer talking to his children," said Esther.

"So what?" replied Marvin, rudely.

"He said wonderful things would happen if they ate their vegetables," said Esther. "So why not try some?"

That night Marvin crept into
the vegetable patch.

He wasn't sure which vegetables to
eat, so he ate a bit of everything.

When Marvin woke up the next morning, something wonderful had happened.

He wasn't blue any more!

His legs were green like leeks.

His tail was orange like a carrot.

His back was as red as a tomato.

His tummy was purple like beetroot. And his face was as yellow as sweetcorn!

"You look amazing!" said the cock.
"Terrific!" said the horse.

"Fabulous!" said the sheep.

"Tremendous!" said the cow.

Marvin was astonished.

None of the animals
had ever been kind to him before.

Mrs Pig was so proud she puffed
up to twice her size and snorted
like a steam train.

A brand new feeling crept over
Marvin. "I feel happy!" he cried.

And guess what?

Marvin turned pink!

Hopscotch has been specially designed to fit the requirements of the National Literacy Strategy. It offers real books by top authors and illustrators for children developing their reading skills.

There are five other Hopscotch stories to choose from:

Plip and Plop
Written by Penny Dolan, illustrated by Lisa Smith
Plip and Plop are two pesky pigeons that live in Sam's grandpa's garden. And if anyone went out, Plip and Plop got busy... Sam has to think of a way to get rid of them!

The Queen's Dragon
Written by Anne Cassidy, illustrated by Gwyneth Williamson
The Queen is fed up with her dragon, Harry. His wings are floppy and his fire has gone out! She decides to find a new one, but it's not quite as easy as she thinks...

Flora McQuack
Written by Penny Dolan, illustrated by Kay Widdowson
Flora McQuack finds a lost egg by the side of the loch and decides to hatch it. But when the egg cracks open, Flora is in for a surprise!

Naughty Nancy
Written by Anne Cassidy, illustrated by Desideria Guicciardini
Norman's little sister Nancy is the naughtiest girl he knows. When Mum goes out for the day, Norman tries hard to keep Nancy out of trouble, but things don't quite go according to plan!

Willie the Whale
Written by Joy Oades, illustrated by Barbara Vagnozzi
Willie the Whale decides to go on a round-the-world adventure – from the South Pole to the desert and even to New York. But is the city really the place for a big, friendly whale?